Mustache Baby

Bridget Heos • Illustrated by Joy Ang

Clarion Books | Houghton Mifflin Harcourt | Boston New York

CLARION BOOKS
215 Park Avenue South, New York, New York 10003

Clarion Books is an imprint of Houghton Mifflin Harcourt Publishing Company.

www.hmhbooks.com

The text in this book was set in Tweed.
The illustrations in this book were executed digitally.
Book design by Sharismar Rodriguez

Library of Congress Cataloging-in-Publication Data
Heos, Bridget.
Mustache baby / Bridget Heos ; [illustrations by] Joy Ang.
p. cm.
Summary: Baby Billy is born with a mustache, and his parents
must figure out if it's a good-guy mustache or a bad-guy mustache.

ISBN 978-0-547-77357-5 (hardcover)

[1. Babies—Fiction. 2. Behavior—Fiction. 3. Mustaches—Fiction.
4. Humorous stories.] I. Ang, Joy, ill. II. Title.
PZ7.H4118Mu 2013
[E]—dc23   2012008155

Manufactured in China
SCP 10 9 8 7 6 5
4500455080

To Josh
—J.A.

For my boys,
Johnny, Richie, & J.J.
—B.H.

Congrats

When Baby Billy was born,
his family noticed something odd:

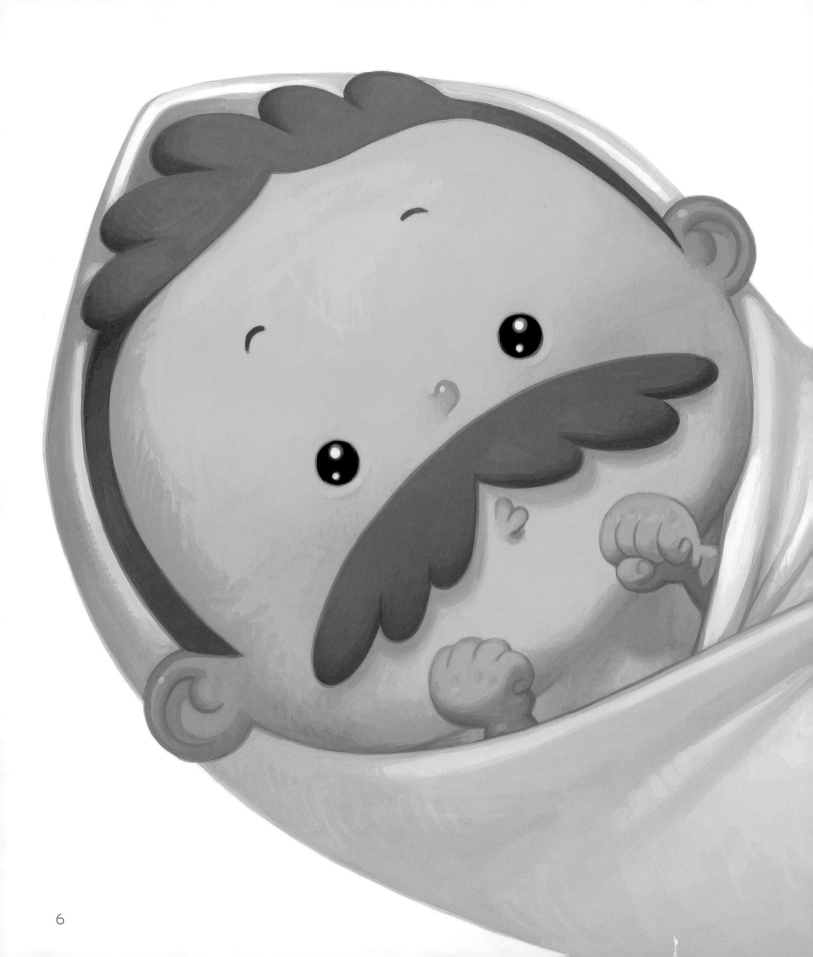

He had a

mustache.

"What does this mean?" his mother asked.

"Well, it depends," the nurse said. "You'll have to wait and see whether it is a good-guy mustache or a bad-guy mustache."

At first, it was plain to see that Billy's mustache was noble and just. He tamed a bucking bronco and became a **COWBOY**.

He always protected his cattle . . .

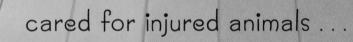
cared for injured animals . . .

and mended broken fences.

After setting things right
on the range, Billy rode off
to become:

A SPANISH PAINTER.

A ringleader.

A **SWORD FIGHTER.**

And finally . . .

a **MAN OF THE LAW,**
for his neighborhood desperately needed him.

With his cop badge, Billy was one tough hombre.

He stopped speeders . . .

outlawed poker . . .

and caught thieves red-handed.

Everyone loved having Officer Billy around.

But a funny thing happened.
As Billy got bigger . . .

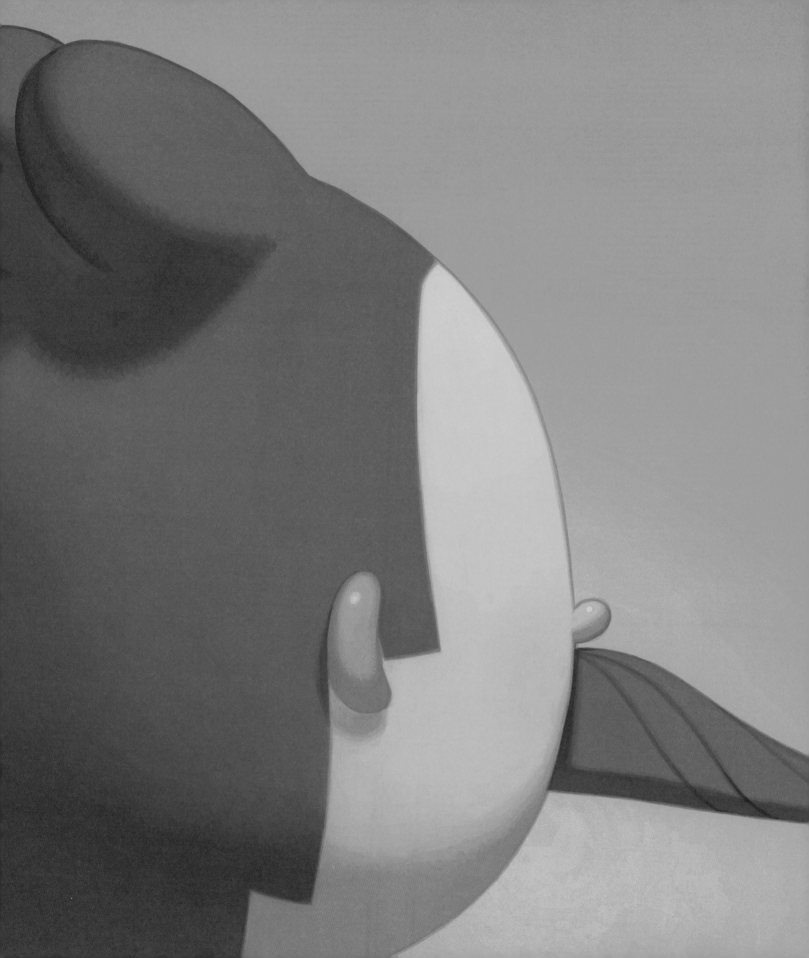

his mustache grew and curled up
at the ends.

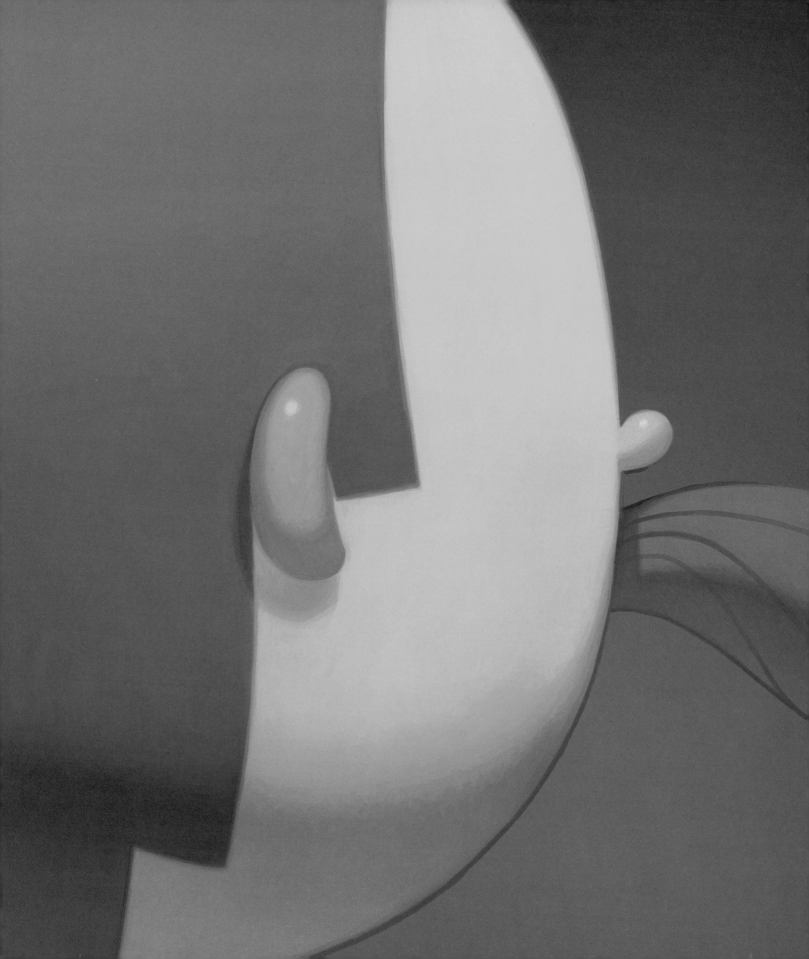

His parents' worst fears were
realized. Billy had a . . .

BAD-GUY
mustache.

Billy's disreputable mustache
led him into a life of dreadful crime.
He became:

A cat burglar.

A CerEAL cRiMiNAL.

And a **TRAIN ROBBER** so heartless
that he even stole the tracks.

But when he planned the biggest heist
of all—a bank robbery—

his getaway car wasn't fast enough.

He got caught . . .

and thrown in jail.

Jail is no place for a baby.
Even a baby with a mustache.

Billy tried to be strong, but
he did shed a few tears.

After ages and ages, Billy regretted his treacherous thievery. He wished that his evil mustache would go away.

At last, his mother busted him out of jail.

"There, there," she said. "Everybody has a bad-mustache day now and then."

"Let's dry your tears," his father said. "The new neighbors have a baby your age. He's coming over to play."

DING-DONG